INTERPOLATED STORIES

INTERPOLATED STORIES

DAVID ROSE

First published in the UK in 2022 by Confingo Publishing

249 Burton Road, Didsbury, Manchester M20 2WA
www.confingopublishing.uk

All images © Leah Leaf 2022
Typesetting by John Oakey
Printed by TJ Books Limited

A CIP catalogue record for this book is available from the British
Library

ISBN 978-1-7399614-6-6

2 4 6 8 10 9 7 5 3 1

CONTENTS

ACKNOWLEDGEMENTS

The following stories were first published in their original, uninterpolated versions: 'Like It' and 'Empire' in *Front&Centre*; 'Edvard Munch Surveys Staines Bridge' in *em one*; 'Amongst the Corots' in *Tees Valley Writer*; 'Cobblers' on the Negative Press London website (www.neg-press.com); 'Smoke' in *Grunt and Groan: The New Fiction Anthology of Work and Sex* (Boheme Press, 2002), its later, interpolated version appearing in *Confingo* 11 (Spring 2018).

AMONGST THE COROTS //

I point three Japanese toward the Titians, resume my seat, watch for Magda.

I rub my ear-ring **?** between finger and thumb, hoping that will conjure her. It does in a way. I'd never have worn it if she hadn't bought it.

It's as well she doesn't come today, I know. In the Sculpture Room, we could duck behind a Henry Moore. Here, there's nowhere for a smeary greeting. That wouldn't put Magda off, but if Arthur saw us, he'd be down on me like a ton of Carl Andres. I can't afford another Disciplinary.

An academic tourist party rounds the corner. The murmur of innumerable BAs. I retreat to the Impressionists, stand up close to a Seurat, play join-the-dots.

My left shoe squeaks as I walk back to the Nineteenth Century. I'm pleased with that. I spent hours finding a pair that squeak. I powder them nightly with talcum. Maxwell says sweat softens the leather and they lose their squeak. He reckons to have the loudest shoes in the Post-Renaissance, but I think mine give him a run for his money.

There is still no sign of Magda.

Camille's **?** not here yet either. He comes most afternoons. Sits on a bench for half an hour, staring at a painting. Just one, a different one each day. Always in a corduroy suit. Silk breast-pocket hankie, brogues. Probably spends his evenings breakdancing to Perry Como records.

Maxwell claims to have seen him crying once, but you can't entirely trust Maxwell. ('Camille' was his idea, too – after Pissarro.) **puerile but**

I check the thermo-hygrograph. It records humidity; a fever chart of sticky breath, a measure of their ecstasy. I'm on lates today, so I have a long afternoon break. I decide to go out.

Crossing to the Square, I almost collide with a cycle courier. He brakes, swerves, swears, nearly dropping his walkie-talkie, then pedals off, humped over the handlebars. In his Lycra shorts and fluorescent crash-hat he looks like a seal with a beachball. I don't bother to swear back, today.

I go into Muswell's and bag a table. We meet here for coffee or a Sol, usually when I come off duty. She's not here, though.

I order an egg and spinach salad. It stares back at me like a Van Gogh landscape. And the music's not loud enough, I can't feel the atmosphere. I leave and walk down Craven Street.

I wander into the Embankment Gardens, builder's sand in my shoes, and make for our tree. It was behind this tree that we first fucked, a quick stand-up job, hidden by the shrubbery. Magda said she felt like one of the Sabine women, but it was **in the open, in a London park? for God's sake. just for a lame joke**

I run my hand over the trunk. The bark feels rough, gritty. I leave it and sit on the bench.

There are some saplings across the garden. One has been pulled over. It slants at about forty degrees. The leaves look feathery as the breeze takes them. Its post has been broken at ground level, but is still strapped to it like a splint. It looks like an entrant in a three-legged race.

Magda and I would walk like that up the Embankment, treading on the cracks. Up to Westminster Pier, to look at the graffiti. Magda liked to see the layers building up. She said it was like an Abstract Expressionist. One day she brought an airbrush and wrote **POLLOCKS ? bloody original**

Magda.

This sounds stupid but, I don't even know if that's her name.

The third time she came to the gallery, she let the others go on, then asked my name. I told her and asked hers. She said, 'Call me Magda,' winked, and went to catch up the group. I looked at the painting she had been standing under. It was a Mantegna, of Christ, Mary Magdalene and the Virgin Mary. I realised she had her hair done to look like Mary Magdalene.

She changes her hairstyle every week. I have to guess what she has copied. After Mantegna, it was a chestnut rinse Rossetti. Then a black spiky Picasso, then short and blonde like Monroe – her Warhol. Then what she called her Van Gogh – brushed over one ear.

I don't know what her latest one is.

Maybe I won't recognise her.

The sun is dropping.

I empty the sand from my shoes and cross the park, past the splinted tree, to watch the river.

There's a group of cranes across the water. I suppose they must have been there before. Strutted legs yellow, but silvered in the sunlight.

I watch them slowly wheel and nod.

I imagine them suddenly taking off, as if disturbed, flocking against **clever pun but doesn't ring true**

I walk quickly back up Craven Street and across Trafalgar Square. I usually skirt the Square. I hate the thought of my uniform being spotted by tourists and pigeons. But I feel drawn to the fountains. I want to take off my shoes and paddle, or jump right in.

I trail my hand for a moment; the water's cold.

Maxwell's off this afternoon. I ask Eric if there was any sign of Magda. He says no, but Camille's been in. As a matter of form I ask which picture it was today. The Corot in the corner.

It's relatively quiet. I sit here undisturbed, massaging my sinuses. The dryness of the air plays them up. Occupational hazards in any job, I suppose.

A group of students gaggle round in whispers. I rub my ear-ring, but she's not among them.

Two of them sit on the dehumidifier cabinet. I hurry to clear them off. I suggest the bench, but they sit on the floor, cross-legged, and giggle. They all have sketch pads and pastels, and copy a Daumier. I watch them as they work, absorbed, huddled, their heads ducking up and down, like a nest of fledglings.

I think of the cranes, and the fountains.

I get up and cross to the corner, to the Corot, and look.

Jean-Baptiste-Camille Corot. The Leaning Tree Trunk. Hardly a trunk, no more than a sapling, really.

Close to, it's so – delicate. The foliage is feathery, the sky, clouds creamy, hazing the hills. You can't make out where the sky merges into the lake. There's something about the light, so cool you could bathe in it. I stand closer and closer, swallowed. **? too aware, I'm not convinced**

I step back. Eric is watching me. I turn my head and pretend to sneeze, blowing my nose.

Fortunately a Japanese fires a flashgun, and Eric spins off like an Exocet. I walk back to my seat.

The students have finished, are packing up, comparing copies. That always seemed a waste of time to me; you can buy perfectly good prints in the gallery shop.

I don't think the Daumier is as good as the Corot. Less delicate. It's nice though. I'll go and have a closer look later. Tomorrow, I think.

There's a portrait in the next room. *Madame Moitessier.* Brown hair, drawn back, with a flounce of lace and ribbon. I wonder if Magda's seen it. Maybe she's already used it. Her Ingrey look?

She won't come now.

I'll find a late-night heel bar on the way home; buy some shoe creme. Kill the squeak. Not the ending I expected; more subtle than I remembered.

No wonder it was never bloody published though. Even as juvenilia it would be trite. Yet I was approaching middle age when I wrote it.

After all, what does it amount to?

A young man, infatuated by promise, is jolted into an appreciation of the art around him, identifying, consciously or not, with an older man, a foppish aesthete, and taking a step toward maturity, allowing readers some fun at the expense of both.

But the implications I find troubling. An equivalence is drawn between the supposed loneliness of the aesthete and the jilted infatuation of the narrator. But *Camille* is just a function of the plot, a straw man, a hollow man, a measure of the youth's progress toward manhood. All supposition, founded on the threadbare tenets of narratology.

For there is no possible equivalence. Consider the situation of the narrator: he has his youth, his friends and colleagues, his work, that friendly toad. What does he – I mean narrator, author – know of Camille? What are we led to surmise? From his attire:

his position in the class spectrum. From his concentration: a belief in the redemptive power of art. From his supposed lachrymosity: an essential loneliness.

But maybe he was in disguise, from himself even? Maybe he was an art historian, member of the Arts Club, even the Groucho? A life teeming with friends, lovers, colleagues, gossip. Maybe his tears were of frustration, disenchantment at art's lack of transcendence. Maybe he would respond more positively to Bacon's dogs than Corot's trees.

The one thing we can be sure of, beyond any surmise, is the essential loneliness. Because of his age.

For is he of an age; he is of that age that individuates, that clarifies loneliness with realisation, that brings desire not for death, which is community, but for oblivion, the second death, the urge to be, by the mercies of St Beckett, both gone and forgotten, for the cosmic fabric to heal immaculately.

There was a woman, I remember that. But older, much older. And later. And *smeary greetings* came into it, as I recall. And an obsession with the softness of a cheek, the down on an upper lip, a web of wrinkles round the eyes. And a cocksure mastery; a harbour of trust then the pull of the tide, a voluptuous self-destruction unheeding the needless hurt.

The consolation of art is precisely this: its insistent barb, its gloating nudge, its reminder of imperfection, contingency; that any painting could have been different, often was, before overpainting. Arbitrariness without arbitration, original sin with no atonement. Corot's trees, Courbet's peasants, Bacon's dogs... voluptuous isolation, and the ragged edge.

How explain all that to our ungallant gallerist, his jejune author?

Leave them be, allow Time's attrition to do its work?

Find a late-night tie bar, buy a cravat?

Better yet: have done; DELETE.

EMPIRE

He is fifth in the queue now, one clerk serving. He pats his pocket. The giro still in the envelope to protect the print. He reads the notices, the Customer Charter. No one should wait longer than five minutes. It's OK. Five minutes is OK. He can wait. He can control his sweat, control his nerves. He controls them with anger. He thinks of oil, of sugar, the cane trade, slave trade. He turns up the flame. It's a trick. He was taught it by Hoonved. They don't really concern him. It's a trick. But it works. He's calm.

He's fourth in the queue.

And Harsi has the car. He'll be waiting in the car park. No sweat. It's harder having to use the train. More exposed. Stephen was taken at the station by the Bennies. You're trapped there. With the car you have a chance.

Drive back to Hoonved. Hand him the money. Watch him count it, enter it into his ledger. Slowly count out and crimp their share. Toss the coins into a drawer. Lean back in his chair, close his eyes, smile, like he's blind. Did well, cunts. Verr well. Screwed them like they screwed your country, yes? Sweet. Suddenly upright, lighting a panatella. Dismiss.

The first excursus of interrogation must be toward establishing which empire(s) delineate our parameters, whose empires fit our categories: Roman? Incan? Ottoman? Spanish, British? Chinese, Portuguese? Then to determine what to do with those that don't conform to our paradigms: Athenian? Lithuanian? Ghanaian or Mandingo? through the back streets of Windsor. Past the barracks. Soldiers of the queen. Up to the castle. Past Queen Victoria, serene and grumpy. Like his grandmother. The bronze weathered to the same colour. He likes to think of that. And of the castle. He knew it from the postage stamps. Solid. A fortress. In the bright day, festooned with tourists. But at night, the granite tower black, the high small windows blazing slits, juju eyes.

And the horses.

Late from Hoonved's, practising signatures, they had seen the police, stopping the traffic, speaking into car windows. He had been scared. Harsi had wanted to reverse, get away. He had used Hoonved's trick, face them.

Then they saw the horses. At full gallop, sweat-streaked in the yellow light. One grazed the car, snapping off the wing mirror. He saw its eyes, smelt its fear. He twisted to watch it, its rhythm broken, energy gathered, knotted, as it frisked across the path of a car, tried to jump it sideways and was hit. Watched it shivering in pain then slowly stiffen.

Harsi swearing lightly under his breath as the traffic began to move like a breaking logjam. As they cleared the town, out toward Winkworth, they could see the glow of the fire.

Third now. A *mukadde*, then a *mweru musajja*, a whitey, with a parcel. The *mukadde* is counting her money, not like the clerks do it but one by one, putting them all the right way up, Queen's head facing up. The clerk sits watching her. She's old too. Granny braids, metal half-moons. Dumpy. Regal. He thinks soon she'll be the other side of the counter, collecting her own pension. The *mukadde* has finished counting, put the money into a purse, purse into a handbag, handbag into a trolley. As she starts to move off, he sees it. A loop of black cable behind the screen. He follows the arc of the loop. It's there, above and to the right of the clerk's head, on the glass shelf, hidden between two piles of leaflets. This is not routine. Little offices don't have routine surveillance. This is not **two countervailing tendencies exerting a torsion on our discourse: inclusivity – defining colonialism as any act of aggression by one state against another and resulting in conquest of land, which would allow almost every people to claim colonized status at some historical juncture; or exclusivity – concentrating on a specific century and a specific empire, normatively selecting the British, possibly the French. Either choice will distort our paradigms, predetermine the discursive telos, and** Whitey has put his parcel on the scales. There's time. Just pat his pocket, swear, walk out like he's forgotten his wallet or whatever. There's time. Probably it's a fisheye lens but it won't have got him full face yet. Keep calm, turn, ease out. He starts to sweat, forehead beading like a beer from the fridge. He ignites the hatred, Hoonved's voice looping through his head. Whitey has his stamps now, picks up his change. Instead of moving to the end of the counter where there's a sponge damper, Whitey sticks them on as he stands there, licking them like pussy, smoothing them with the ball of his hand. A tenpence, a fivepence, then a five pound. He recognises the brown engraving of Windsor Castle. They're all on now, smoothed, firmed again – Whitey don't trust his own country's glue – the parcel **archival production of that cultural inscription of self-consciousness on a post-colonized society that mutates into the post-colonial per se presupposes an intellectual elite of sufficient maturity to effect a mediation in** takes the giro from its envelope, slides it through together with his fake ID. Hoonved's voice is galloping through his head. The clerk leans forward, her hair metallic grey, sculpted on her head. Sunlight off a passing car catches her glasses, blanks out her eyes like she's blind, her face a mask. Slits. He thinks of Hoonved, moonfaced, smiling behind his glasses. Thinks of the softness of his throat.

He ste**counter the charge – made either by or on behalf of those societies – that this is a Western appropriation of Third World culture for Postmodernist discourse, representing an analogous but more insidious form of empire-building;**

COBBLERS

He has never liked Christmas. It's his busiest time – booked almost daily, sometimes double-booked, for the weeks of the holiday; his peak earning-period. Nonetheless

He gets tired, goes flat, effervesces less and less, has to act the part more. This is the second of the day, the fourth this week.

It's almost set up now: the puppet kiosk in the lounge, the bouncy castle inflated on the patio, his skeleton suit on under a tracksuit, the black curtain hung over the door. Now the task he has come to dread.

He takes a balloon, stretches the neck between two fingers, slips it over the pump, pumps with his foot, looking away. The balloons are raw, resistant. He used to re-use them. Snap off the clip, allow to deflate, store in a box. Waste not, want not.

Now he finds the deflated ones worse. In their shrivelled state they resemble even more closely spermatozoa, statically swimming in their cardboard box.

He can hear the children, still at table in the dining room, the noise ebbing and flowing with the serving of the courses. He bunches some balloons, garlands the kiosk, arranges others in piles around the room.

He strips off his tracksuit, pushes it under the kiosk, and he's ready, just in time. He disappears behind the open door as they file into the lounge.

They are looking around, expecting someone to be there, disconcerted to find there isn't. He feels their expectancy, allows it to mount as he pulls on his skull mask.

One boy kicks into a pile of balloons, followed by some of the others. That's good – it allows him to identify the dominant ones. He waits as the noise and kicking increase, then, as a climax, slams the door shut, standing against it, framed against the black backdrop.

He lets the shrieks die away.

–Are you all friends? Has everyone here got a friend? That's nice, that's good. Everyone needs friends. Don't be like me. I've got nobody. No body.

(Stick to the old stuff, the tried and tested.)

He puts a hand on his chest.

–No, it's sad, that's why I feel sternum. It's not funny, it's not humerus (waggling his arm). All right, laugh if you like, I can take a ribbing.

He pulls a pair of drumsticks from his back pocket, starts tapping his neck.

–Quiet, please. I'm playing the clavicles. I can't play the organ, I haven't any.

He has them now, taking them with him. He takes a saucer from his other pocket, holds it below his knee.

–Here, tibia, tibia. What? Of course it will. Look, the saucer's empty now. Oh yes it did. You think I'm telling fibulas? Now, meet Elvis. Right, down to the windy plains of Ilium. Never heard of Ilium? You haven't been doing your Homerwork, have you?

This is above them, he's in danger of losing them, although the inquisitive ones will look it up later. He needs to win them back.

He picks up the xylophone, starts to play 'Dem Bones, Dem Bones', leads them in a conga twice round the room, wends towards the kiosk, ducks inside and pulls on the diving suit.

It gives him time to calm himself. For the numbers in the room have suddenly swelled. Amongst the children crowding the kiosk he sees the hosts of the unborn jostling for attention, standing on tiptoe or shyly watching.

He dons the helmet, slowly rises above the ledge. The crowd has shrunk back to the corporeal. He breathes deeply in the helmet as he works his fingers into the rubber octopus.

–Don't forget the diver.

Even *he* doesn't remember ITMA but the catchphrase still works. They are fully attentive. There is one boy in particular, about eight, with a reddish glint in his hair and wonder-filled eyes, enchanted by the underwater scene in the mock aquarium, the iridescent shells and ceramic crabs. Quiet, studious, not an alpha male. He feels a kinship with the boy, decides to play to him. He points into the pebbles.

–Look, there's Algy.

The boy responds, laughs, understanding the joke, leading the others.

In every party he can pick out one, the one his wife would take to, take as her own, the one who would spark off the old regrets.

He tries to shut it off, concentrate on the slow-motion movement of the octopus. It's something he'd like to have discussed with her, but he's never felt up to it. A problem shared is a problem doubled. He has simply passed it off as one of life's ironies. 'Cobblers usually go unshod.'

He finds himself drifting to the fathomless depths, working the puppets on automatic pilot. He has to pull himself back to the surface, back to the eyes.

–These? They're bookends. This is the Continental Shelf. Where'd he come from? Cheeky urchin.

He's relaxing into it again, the routine second nature – the nervous wreck, the ice cream jelly fish, the struggle to open the sunken chest ('No good, won't budge. You need mussels for this job'). Now he starts building up to the climax.

He manoeuvres the octopus toward his neck, flicking the tentacles at his helmet. Some of the children shout a warning.

–What's that? Can't hear with this helmet on. Who's attacking? What? Aaaargh.

He whips the tentacles so they twist round his neck, prolonging the battle as long as he dares, judging the point at which the tension will fall, then picks up a harpoon, spears the octopus repeatedly, has it flounder and thrash and sink out of sight.

–There. He's an octogon.

He gathers a handful of foil-wrapped chocolate coins from among the pebbles.

–Look. Six squid. No, they're pieces of eight. Doubloons. Doubloons, doubloons, dem dub-loons. Hurray.

He throws them by the handful out into the crowd.

They shout and laugh as they catch them, scuffling over the ones on the floor.

He comes out from the kiosk, wades in **the dusk, a stirless movement** among them, leads them in a slow-motion dance around the room **of animulation** making gurgling noises inside the helmet. He thinks he hears, through the helmet, a soundless clamour beneath the shouting. But **fleeting, issue of an ordaining Love, skittering between beguiling trifles, thus drawn** he's safe now, it's almost **by the life, the warmth, the light through the window** over.

He pulls off his helmet, and from a pocket in the suit takes a packet of hat pins.

–Right. Line up. Harpoons at the ready. Go.

They attack the piled balloons with gusto, a frenzy of stabbing, kicking, shrieking. Three boys fight to burst the last one. Now they all stand, keyed up, expectant of anticlimax.

–On to the bouncy castle.

They cheer, swarm through the French windows, throw themselves on to the castle.

He relaxes now. Picks up his dustpan and brush, sweeps up the shredded rubber. One balloon is still intact, shrivelled rather than burst, a faulty seal maybe. He picks it up with finger and thumb. It reminds him, even more forcibly than usual, of the sperm depicted on the poster in the clinic, a last warning before the final decision. 'Are You Sure?'

He drops the balloon into the dustpan, finishes sweeping, checks the corners. Now he can pack up, dismantle the kiosk **seeking ingress** take down the black curtain, take off the diving suit, start loading the van.

He checks on the children, still squealing and jumping. He picks out the boy, her boy; he's fully integrated into the crowd, the laughter.

He goes back to the van, sits inside, allowing them an extra half hour, to wind down gradually.

After twenty minutes, the castle is deserted, the garden quiet. He goes back to deflate the castle, fingers the valve, realises the extent of his tiredness, the allure of the castle. He lies down, undulating.

He finds himself shivering in the wind, newly risen. He gets the diving suit from the van, pulls it back on, resettles himself on the castle.

Each stir of wind animates it. He imagines himself drifting with the tide, then descending, into the green amniotic depths, the silence.

But even the depths, the oceanic trenches, teem with life, with prodigal birth, driving him back to the surface, the single atmosphere, the deserted garden.

He keeps perfectly still.

The wind has pushed back the clouds to reveal **the sensible cosmos** the moon. Its light shivers through the chill air. *Silver chains of moonbeams dancing.* In the house there were swags of paperchains, handmade from paper twisted and gummed, probably by the children. Long spirals looping from the picture rails. Blue and gold to match the decor.

He had seen a programme on DNA, computer-animated, the floppy ladder wound into every cell, spiralling back over generations, on into the future, endless sequence, a reverse-lottery tickertape endlessly ***Better thus*** reproduced.

He looks up at the moon, imagines himself there, his gravity-less tread in his rubber suit. ***Better not***

Are the footsteps still there from three decades ago? Or blown away by the solar winds, the moondust resettled in the whispered cosmic surf? ***Better to have never***

It's time, he knows, to collapse the castle, stow it in the van, drive home, put on one more act, describing the evening to his wife: the house, the children, as many as he can remember, the acts, the applause; relive it all over again.

And again.

SMOKE

I don't now. Haven't done since the fire. Sounds daft, doesn't it, 'the fire'. Like a postman saying 'the letter'.

She never liked me being in the service – didn't like the shifts, didn't like the danger. I tried to tell her, there's no danger, we know what we're about. We're trained. I tried to explain.

She blamed the job more and more. I think by then it was an excuse. I think she'd have drunk anyway.

I wouldn't have said it was a vocation exactly. But it was, a challenge, like. I loved it. If I'd had to choose, well, I did have to choose, but it was no choice, really.

I kept wanting to tell her, but, I didn't have the words. I kept trying to explain, that I didn't have the words.

Then the more she drank the harder it was.

I was over it by then. I thought I was. Settled. Digs but, comfortable.

We were nearly through our watch when the shout came. Routine call-out, domestic job, chip pan, probably.

I was in the back of the engine, doing up my jacket, I didn't hear the address over the radio.

It *was* the kitchen, but not the stove. It was centred on the draining board, the one she'd kept wanting me to replace. The flame was spreading across the board and up the wall, although given the open top window, it ought to have reached ceiling height in the estimated time of combustion. I didn't remark on it though.

We'd rolled out two lines, just to be sure, but we didn't need the second. Except that I noticed a secondary inflammation under the draining board, between the wall and washing machine.

We buried it, doused down the walls and ceiling and started rolling up.

I said I'd stay and do the final check. Andy'd realised. I knew he'd cover for me.

When I went back in, she was in the dining room, her skirt off, blouse unbuttoned. It was still tight on her. I remembered I'd bought it for her, so it was a size too small to start with, plus she'd put on weight.

She pulled her blouse off, swagged it over the settee. In its draught I caught an odour beneath the alcohol. Lighter fuel.

I said, for God's sake, why didn't you just phone me? She said, I tried, you're never there, you were *never* there.

I suppose it was the adrenalin. All the lads find that at a fire, especially after a long spell of no shouts.

And she was still a beautiful woman. I mean, I still felt something for her. I still

She took me into the spare bedroom – it was the one she seemed to be using now.

She pulled my braces over my shoulders, worked my waterproofs down, then, on her knees, unbuckled my belt. I pulled her up, sat her on the bed while I undressed – I always preferred to undress myself.

She was leaning back on the bed on her elbows, her bra off, legs drawn up.

I stood there. She sat on the bed's edge, leaned forward and took me between her breasts. Her movements were clumsy, but I didn't think it was just the drink.

I leaned over her, held her head. I could smell the smoke in her hair.

I pushed her back across the bed, moved down her body, and I could smell the smoke on her skin, and even stronger between her legs. I could detect her own scent, beneath the smoke, but it was like, from a distance, far off, different.

I looked up to her. I thought I could see reflected in the white of her underbreasts the fire, flames pleating and folding. It turned out to be chafe marks from her bra, but at first, before I realised, it sort of spurred me on, my tongue going deeper and deeper.

I moved back up, kissed her neck. I came into her, and it was   it was like coming home but, coming home for the first time.

She had her face in the pillow, she seemed to be crying.

Andy started honking outside. I dressed and looked over at her. She was still shuddering, but as if in her sleep.

I tiptoed out.

Andy just nodded, started the engine.

Right bloody hoo-ha when the report went in. I offered to resign if they took it no further. They agreed.

Broke up the watch. Bloody good watch. Best bloody watch in the station. Close, that's why. We didn't play cards much, we knew each other's weaknesses so well. Close.

Waste. Somehow the council still found out. Rehoused her on another estate, rough. Dealing, fencing.

I don't know where she lives now.

I saw her once in McDonald's, with **political pyrotechnics of selfhood whose only eventuation is not**

visibility but legibility, a legibility that retracts back into invisibility; of the ladies. She'd just dyed her hair. In the ladies. It was still dripping, down her face, her neck.

The bloke scarpered when he **performativity decreed by the patriarchal structures thus reinforced, the quest for an illusory 'selfhood' shown up – manifest – as**

Waste.

Best bloody watch in **self*ish,* an attempt at 'individuation' instead of** to a few newspapers, packing crates. Have to be careful, being a warehouse.

Close my eyes. Inhale. Feel the **resistant queering of the dynamics of** mostly nights, but I was always OK on shifts.

Warehouse is cold, though. Even in summer, cold as a crypt.

LIKE IT

The alley was too narrow. That was the first problem. No way I could get down and turn in, with the angle of the gate. I decided to reverse down, beyond the gate, then forward and turn.

Not so easy. Luckily it's Tuesday, the hangover had settled down, just the throbbing across the forehead, hands steady enough. But I'd only done ten yards when the mirror caught, hit by a window ledge at the exact wrong height. Sheared off. I had to inch down, steer by the bumps.

I crawled past the gate, swung and in. I heard cheering. The post-demo crew, about a dozen, stood round the gatepost, some of them pantomiming, legs crossed. I leaned out of the cab, asked where they wanted it. The foreman pointed to a clearing in the rubble by the far fence.

That was the second problem. Negotiate the rubble. They'd started bulldozing the bricks, heaping them into piles, but they'd not got as far as the fence. I had to drive over the mounded rubble, keeping an equilibrium. I just knew the unit would topple. They say there's a minimum angle for that to happen, but. Sod's law, forever valid.

I was lucky. But I felt I needed a shit myself by then.

Third problem was, the site they'd chosen wasn't in my judgement sufficiently even. They'd levelled it off, but not a big enough area for the base of the unit. I measured it out. Enough space to site it but there was a dip at one end. Can't afford any risk of tilting these.

Thunderbirds – the industrial wing – advertise in the construction trade press under the slogan 'Jakes In Two Shakes'. This was going to take a sodding sight more than two.

The foreman waved the bulldozer over, got the others crushing bricks to fill in the dip, then the driver pounded them down. I managed to find a beam about the right length, laid it across, checked with the spirit level.

They dug out some of the rubble, flattened it again, added a bit more, until I felt satisfied. I let the jack down, craned the unit over, lowered it into place, checked with the plumb line, gave them the nod. There was another round of cheering.

Foreman suggested a brew, so they could test it. We drank it by the bonfire of splintered rafters.

Three years I've been with Thunderbirds. Longest time I've stayed in one job. Keeps Wendy happy. Regular hours, no shifts. It's the shifts she can't stand, never knowing when I'll be home. Likes me out of the house during the day. She's got an afternoon job. In a florist's. Brings home the leftovers, damaged flowers, 'bruised' is the trade term. Every day I find squashed marguerites or bent strelitzias in my darts trophy.

It's the mornings. Hates me around her feet. Best job I had, best for me, worst for her, was the brewery, driving the beer tankers. Except I'd say, no, I wasn't the driver, I rode shotgun. Good line for breaking the ice, at parties or the pub. It was nights. I'd finish and be home by ten, having a breakfast-supper while she watched morning telly. Niggled her. I said, why not swap to mornings? No, they had someone doing mornings. I said, you don't really need to work. Do something else to take you out. Take up charity work. She said, 'I did that when I married you.' I let it ride.

Riding shotgun. Actually, I've got a good line with this job. People ask me what I do, I say, 'professional piss-taker'. That's down the pub. One of Wendy's friends, I have to say something like 'sanitation consultant', or use the company phrase, 'customised sewer-leverage'. Though I'm often tempted.

Fact is, though, I've put in for a transfer, to the so-cial wing. They cover garden parties, country-house dos, outdoor performances. They advertise that side of the business in the posh papers, *Country Life*, *The Lady*. They call it their 'prêt-à-cabinets' service, it's French, or else, 'bespoke waste solutions'. I wouldn't call it bespoke myself. It's hardly made-to-measure. They just have various outsides that clip over the ba-sic units, like the Elizabethan Half-timbered or the wrought-iron Victorian Folly, all in fibre glass. I was told there's even a police box for Doctor Who conven-tions, but that might be a wind-up.

Different uniform. Not overalls, black trousers, white shirt, black bow tie, on elastic. And you're in-spected before you go out.

Mind you, my overalls are always spotless. She even irons them. One thing about Wendy, you can't fault her laundry.

I haven't told her yet. And it's not for her sake I'm doing it. I mean, she'd be pleased. Except for the hours, being seasonal. Summer is peak time, of course. De-pending on distance, it means an early set-off, then on duty for the duration, superintending the plum-bage and flow, dismantling late at night. Long days. But then maybe a few days off. That'll be the problem.

Well, she'll have to like it or lump it. As I said, it's not for her, or the money. Or the uniform. Totally not the uniform. Worse than wearing a bloody suit.

No, it's because of last summer.

What with the recession, the building slump, bloke called Collier waiting for a hernia job, they asked me to help on the social wing. 'On secondment,' they said. Out in Surrey, open-air theatre. I thought, why not, bit of greenery, try a few local ales.

It was beyond Godalming, grounds of some country house, small. I drove the unit, Ron took the tanker. The unit was the 'Half-timbered', so Ron put money on it being Shakespeare. He was right.

Came off the A3 too soon, got stuck in Guildford, but we still got there by ten. Nice flat site. Measured out, trenched in the pipes, settled the unit, screened off the tanker, all connected up by one. We looked over the grounds. Stage was a large flattened mound, grassed over, steps at the back. A few trees behind, then proper woods behind them.

We took the truck, drove back to the pub we'd passed on the way in, had a bevy of the local brew – called Old Brock, should have come with a spoon – drove back.

Some of the actors were there by then, doing a last

run-through, which meant, with their nerves, I suppose, we had to do the same. All pumping through OK.

It was all working so smoothly in fact that when the performance began, I started watching it. Bits of it, between restocking the soap and towels.

It was called *As You Like It*. The programme I picked up called it a comedy but I didn't get many jokes, and it ended with mass marriage, which seems more like a tragedy. Plus I got confused with the disguises. And there were two characters both called Jakes but spelt French, and one of them never appeared. Ron was there when the other Jakes came on. He said, 'Oh, he'll be off in two shakes.' Luckily he fucked off himself then to see if his bow tie would get him in with the bar staff.

We were both kept busy after the end, stocking up, adjusting the pump and water pressure, right until the evening performance was well along. Then they gave us a load of leftovers from the buffet. I took mine and sat on the grass at the side of the stage, tried to follow it. I'd worked out a bit of the plot first time round, now I caught on to some of the speeches. Hard to understand but they sounded lovely the way they said them, sort of musical.

It had been hot all day, bit cloudy, but now the cloud had gone, it was nearing dusk by the end, and in the last bit, last act, as they were all declaring their love and getting hitched in the forest, the moon came up behind the trees at the back, almost full, bright, just like a stage effect, it was magic.

It was after midnight when we **a binary polarity endemic to the pastoral genre, between *civility* and *rusticity,* Shakespeare complexifies, to the point of compromise, that polarity by positing a group of rustics – Duke Senior and his band – who are in actuality civilised, albeit exiled; a compromise that wreaks a disruption – an aporia – to the norms of the genre and of wider societal** sounds soft. But I had to follow it up, I couldn't leave it. I wanted to read the words for myself. I went to the library. Thing is, I'm not good at books. Magazines I'm OK, but books I find a task. Wendy knows that. She saw me reading the library book. She said, 'Is that the comic edition? You should start with lamb's tails.' I didn't know what she meant. I ignored it.

I was getting the hang of it, mostly reading the notes at the bottom, some of them taking up half the page, but they were interesting. And then some of the speeches I remembered, and some I didn't but liked. Someone says, an example, 'How full of briers is the working-day world,' I thought, yeah. And this Orlando says, 'These trees shall be my books, and in their barks my thoughts I'll character,' which reminded me of carving love hearts as a kid.

I don't think though, to be honest, if I'd just read the book, I'd have got much from it. But I could hear the words, see the actors, in my mind, I could see the moon coming up and smell the breeze through the woods, and I think it was all that together, and it seemed to have a meaning, for me.

I read something, too, in the notes, that explained something, an incident, a run-in. I'd had to tighten one of the joints, and as I came round from behind the unit this girl, pretty in a toity way, pushed passed me and got a smudge on her dress from my wrench.

I said sorry – well, you do, don't you? But she just looked at me, and then gave a sort of little scream like a long hiccup. Then this bloke, boyfriend, said in a tweedy voice, 'Oh, one of the rude mechanicals.' Snarky cunt. Lucky I didn't lamp him.

Now I know what he was referring to, except he'd got the play wrong, they're in *Midsummer Night's Dream*. But what I'm saying, is, yeah, I'm happy to be one of the rude mechanicals, that's my lot, I'm happy with it. I'm not thinking of going off studying drama, be an actor, write books, even read them. I'll go on being a rude mechanical. But there's a dimension I've been missing, along with the driving and installing and a few beers down the pub, and if I can just get this transfer, I'll **utilises Elizabethan spectators' expectation and acceptance of female characters played by boys, by a performative double bluff, viz. females, played by boys, disguised as men. This cross-dressing doubled – a double-crossing of societal hierarchies – thus uses the liminality of both the genre and the wider convention to destabilise the normative gendering of patriarchal structures** plating him. Foreman was **what degree this is reflected in the phenomenological experience of modern audiences opens up a space for discussion of both gender and homoerotics; feminism and queer theory come to bear alongside New Historicist theories of social circularity to explore** Besides, there's Wendy.

DECRESCENDO

Because I thought at last I was on to something, something settled, suited to my mind, my solipsistic bent, a system I could relax in, luxuriate in, no loose ends, well few loose ends, but congenial.

Because I always believed one should choose one's metaphysics carefully, scrupulously, off-the-peg maybe but adjusted to fit, room for expansion. To that end, *The History of Western Philosophy* became the bible of my impressionable years, the russell of dead ideas flocculating my adolescence. But with that surge of positivity in my twenties – a period of ayers and graces, schlick insistence – I detected, perceived, a certain hand-me-down aspect to it all, like wearing my father's trousers, and disillusion set ***Wisdom dwells with prudence and finds out knowledge of witty inventions*** aridity of that relentless positivism at least led me tangentially to Wittgenstein, the excitement of the stops and ladder, the silence of the spheres, fly in the bottle, bewitchment of the language games. ***is better than rubies*** of age, even bought myself some brogues and tweed jacket, threw out my ties, started to live, confident that the logical kinks would be ironed out; thought, even, of finding a job.

Not the least of the appeal, of the *Tractatus* in particular, was its logical justification of my solipsism, which I had tried to disguise as shyness, but which now required no disguise nor apology – I was granted permission, my solipsism was correct, said Wittgenstein, but could not be stated, only manifested. A weight lifted from my shoulders, a bolstering of my confidence.

So began the years of hesitant expansion, controlled collisions with limited damage, unscathing liaisons, psychic experiment, almost, one could say, happiness.

But in the long terrain of middle life, as the solipsism became loneliness, the cosmic silence ominous, I turned instead to Spinoza. Recurringly drawn to a passage in Wittgenstein concerning pain, prompted by my own, which invited consideration of stones in their capacity – incapacity – to feel pain, thinking, I recall, *fuck off, Ludwig – how can you be so sure stones feel no pain, that my schmerz doesn't extend to die welt?*

I reread the passage in Russell on Spinoza, for whom even stones had souls and presumably pains.

I became surprisingly **very stones will cry out** Spinozan vision – the cosmos as the mind of God. I felt my bounds breached in outward flood, a feeling akin to happiness as I had heard it described. What walks, what rambles followed. I become animated just recalling them, but at the time felt *energised,* felt myself a unit in a cosmic forcefield, the world crackling with intelligence, bristling with sentience, the Pathetic Fallacy fallacious no longer. In my tramps through the copse beyond town I was aware of a current pulsing from tree to tree, xylonic pylons, of sap mingling like lovers' saliva, of **Let the fields be joyful and all the trees of the wood** stones aligned, patterned like iron filings.

Was this, I asked, a discovery of God, this shimmering immanence? It was, at any rate, a discovery of women. There was Carla, whose erythema, when aroused, would spread to her breasts, there was Julia, with the almond eyes of a Modigliani, there was Marie – or was it Mary – of demure mien and guttural laugh, each one a breach in my psychic dyke, an *abandon* – an expression I had always thought ornamental. So this, I thought, is what they meant.

Looking back, it couldn't last, this... euphoria. We are not made for happiness, perhaps. In a sober lull, I identified the logical flaw: if God *is* the cosmos, the cosmos is God, the strongest inference at most deistic. I was plunged headlong into the old solipsistic loneliness, but with an awakened need for acknowledgement which remained unassuaged, indeed deepened by a gravidating guilt.

Carla, Julia, Marie/Mary – they were not a meeting of minds but a fusion of bodies, on my side at least. Yet avowals were made, and by me, as I remember; I won't say in good faith, for that is to weight judgement. From this metaphysical collapse, could anything be salvaged? Was it to be a return to the ethical silence? Silence was what I desired, though – I felt even the stones condemning me, guilt accruing with no means of expiation.

In the impasse I consulted my dog-eared Russell.

Much of Spinoza, it transpired, had been purloined by Leibniz, but with significant modifications – *modulations* – which afforded some progression. Leibniz is the boy all right, I thought, Leibniz is the body, the bee's knees.

I was struck in particular by his elegant minimalism: the universe reduced to just God and an infinite array of monads – composite, indivisible soul-like entities, self-sufficient units, like so many mirrors reflecting the universe, each monad's peculiar perceptions *pregnant with the future, laden with the past.*

Much of the elegance lay in the solution, by dis-solution, of those perennial problems of causation, dualism, free will, by its dazzling vision of unreacting integers controlled by an intricate pre-established har-mony – synchronised swimming on a cosmic scale.

More personally important, though, were its impli-cations for that bundle of monads comprising my self. Here surely, I thought, is a fully licensed theism. For God, that Ultimate Solipsist, had broken out of His loneliness by bringing forth this teeming universe of monadic actors whose whole raison d'être lay in being perceived by Him.

Here was salvation: God the Spectator, the Ulti-mate Perceiver. Interaction was no longer the point. I was perceived; acknowledgment was unnecessary – I was watched, if not watched over. I remember tell-ing myself (who else was there?) that expiation was a pointless goal, a wild goose chase, barking up the wrong tree (nothing like a good cliché for sedating the conscience), that to be perceived, therefore accepted, just as I am, was enough.

Alas, my conscience refused to be sedated. With the infirmities of age, the firmities of reason gave way, the old solipsistic fears swept back, the self-accusato-ry voices more sibilant. There followed long periods of truculent self-debate (the sound of one hand clapping ***and with all thy getting get understanding*** logical flaw alluded to by Russell, that if monads are unable to interact, remaining locked in solitary isolation, what guarantee that the universe exists, that the mirroring is not a dream?

The final blow was a remark I came across, glossing Bishop Berkeley's *to be is to be perceived* to the effect that self- perception supersedes all outside perception.

That was not my understanding of Berkeley, that was not my idea of Idealism, not my ideal at all. Mindful of Dr Joh***this stone shall be a witness*** a kick in the monads. Existence predicated on the perception of God, and existence validated by self-perception, are two very different kettles of fish. Self-perception was precisely what I was trying to escape, prying introspection allowing of no mitigation, no exoneration, of the accruing guilt.

I lost all interest in a now-clockwork cosmos, craved the penumbra shading to blackness, sought not recognition but an oubliette. For I had come to the blinding realisation that only ***furrows likewise complain thereof.*** **Let the fields be joyful and all the trees of the wood rejoice, for he cometh to judge the earth with his truth.** ***For the stones shall cry out of the wall*** *and the beam out of the timber shall answer it* thou canst not look on iniquity *under a juniper tree: and he requested for himself that he might die* the wind an earthquake *and after the earthquake a fire, and after the fire* sit in my perspex rotunda, open umbrella tipping the ceiling, and write.

UNDER THE PLAN

First he had to renew his licence, *then* on to the mall.

As with all institutional buildings, it was over-heated. So the calipers were cool to his brow as they checked the measure of his temples, but were warming when they measured the lesions he had come to report.

They rechecked the other measurements recorded on his licence: angle and degree of asymmetry of the ears; gap between his eyes; obtrusion of his jaw (suffice to say, a quarter inch more would have disqualified the licence). He was asked about the lesions, livid against the birthmark, and he hinted at the possibility – as yet medically unconfirmed – of their being carcinomas from solar exposure; to which they replied, Well, if you insist on appearing in public...

They asked him to confirm his neutered status.

There was a moment's silence as they updated his phrenological map for the County records, printed off a copy and stapled it to his licence. They stamped that and handed it to him with the *nunc dimittis* 'stay out of the sun, keep to the shade – you'll be less conspicuous'.

He caught a bus to the mall.

He sat at the back, licence brandished as a shield; it was perfectly unnecessary.

He entered the mall from the bus depot, choosing the automatic doors to avoid the temptation of holding the door for fellow ingressors, then by scuttling from shop window to shop window, window-shopping at each, made his way to the benches in the atrium, and relaxed. Blue sky and a sliver of moon manifested themselves through the glass roof.

Under the Plan, he is permitted by licence six hours daily in public view, inclusive of two hours of alms prospecting, which applies to both daylight and artificial illumination; in the dark, he is unrestricted. But darkness is hard to find in suburbia, so he tries to make the most of his time in the open, sopping up the sensible delights of life's cornucopia: the shoe shop across from today's bench, for example, where a pair of powder-blue loafers had him in covetous rapture (though, even if he had the money, why reinforce public prejudice? Best advised to stick with his lace-ups).

Then, a display of stilettos having given him just that erotic charge needed to overcome his shyness, he rose and made his way to the main exit into the High Street.

Sully (for that is his name, though whether birth name or nickname isn't known) was born before the Plan, to a mother who was in her way conventionally attractive. He tended her; he laid her to rest. There will be none to do the same for Sully. But, such is the benevolence of Nature, licensees **KELLOGG'S CORNFLAKES MAKE BETTER BABIES** long lives. Besides, why perpetuate the misery? Why risk mocking infinity? Those vertiginous spaces, those aeons of loneliness – he becomes calmed and excited just by contemplating them.

Meanwhile he has to subsist. The acoustics are better inside the mall but live music there is illegal. So he is here on the outside, spare cap on the pavement, seeded with coins, Hohner to his mouth. (His instrument of choice was the accordion, but the harmonica, between cupped hands, obscures much of his face, to tactical advantage.)

He opens, for the sake of its self-mocking melancholy, with a rendition of 'Summertime' notable for an ironic rubato. Then, after a pause for effect, launches into his standard medley of 'Blue Skies', 'Sunny Side of the Street' and 'I Want to Be Happy'.

In fact, by that juncture, he *is* happy – unfailingly, the music, his absorption of and into the skeins of sound, the fragility and wistfulness, have taken him not out of himself so much as deeper into himself, into that core of being beyond all phrenological reach, into what *we* would describe as a serenity of acceptance.

So much so that he now winds up, and down, with a rendition of 'Ugly Rumours', partly a wry admission, mainly for the hell of it.

Breathless now, in that state of exhilaration and annihilation, he squats on his heels contemplating the paving.

He has registered, during the playing, the clink of coins but has learnt not to acknowledge them – sustaining the introversion of the artist allows him to keep his face obscured. Now, after a decent interval judged by the footfall, he picks up the cap without apparent interest (he thinks that bad form) and heads back into the mall for a breather.

As he approaches the portico, he is accosted by a man, a tweedy gent in highly buffed brogues. Sully instinctively fingers his licence.

'Spirited performance. Most enjoyable. Not enough live music about these days. Welcome change to all this Muzak. The odd bum note only adds to the authenticity, in my opinion.'

Sully concentrates on the polished brogues, cheered by noting a fraying lace.

'Quiet word from a civic conscience, though. I'd find another venue next week if I were you. All this area to be closely vetted. Mall, High Street, castle precincts. The wedding. Just for the day. Word to the wise. Head down, what?'

Sully watches the lace strain as the brogues depart. But the glimmer of hope hardly offsets the discomfort he feels. He has to sit down. He walks rapidly through the mall, head down, headed for his bench of before.

The bench is vacant but now seems exposed. He hurries past, striking deeper into the mall until he reaches the atrium with its oasis of calm for frenetic shoppers: a fountain fringed with potted palms and ferns. He sits abruptly on the tiled surround amidst the foliage, ensconced like a virgin in a Delvaux, and slowly recovers.

He breathes deeply, regularly, as his mother taught him, counting his blessings, reflecting on the effort it must take to be handsome and kempt, that handsome is as handsome does, and that even **Judgment in State of Tennessee v. John Thomas Scopes, Judge John**

T. **Raulston presiding** through the fronds like a lost German soldier **A Civic Biology: Presented In Problems – George William Hunter** to the footsteps from *spreading disease, immorality and crime to all parts of...* heartbeat now slowing *do have the remedy of separating* from its protective sheath *and degenerate race* between thumb and index finger of each hand.

Do you – can you – feel that tear thrilling across the paper, the pieces fluttering like field butterflies to the floor?

Three generations of imbeciles is enough. (Buck v. Bell)

EDVARD MUNCH SURVEYS STAINES BRIDGE

striding its paving, striking his heels, willing the ice-pricked winds to sweep down the centuries and through the railings.

None comes. He grasps the balustrade, listens.

Muttering, indistinct at first.

Mother – Johanna – Jørgen – Laura – Mother – Johanna – Father – Laura...

A crowd of people walking up Clarence Street, faces drained after a day's work. He watches, thinks of *Evening on Karl Johan Street*, the stream of ghostly pedestrians, their faces pressed against the plane. A stab of compassion for his creatures in their two-dimensional existence.

He returns to the living instead; or rather, the dead. Mother, Johanna, Jørgen. The dead beyond our grasp. They take with them their share of our lives, strip us of years, leaving fragments only of our past selves – a button, orchard scents, taste of bitter coffee, cold of a wrought-iron table. Hemmed in to the little of the past they left untouched, and the present. Always the present.

He pockets the names like a rosary, leans over the parapet.

There, down there, the Hythe, the landing place. Built over, now, public houses, white-walled cottages. But there *he* would have landed, to winter, gather strength, allow the wounded rest until the spring, and the harrying could begin again, the close season over.

He, Munch, had ridden the ferry, commanding the prow for the whole of the journey, North Sea spray salting his moustache, travelling via Harwich and Ostend in order to arrive, as he must, at Folkestone, *in this year came Olaf Tryggvason with 93 ships to Folkestone, and harried outside* jostling from the prow to stride, first, down the gangway, listening for the faint **dissolution of the materiality of the sign means the dissolution of history**

and sailed thence to Sandwich, and thence to Ipswich, overrunning the countryside, and so on to Malden...
As the train broke steam out of Ipswich he had let down the window, leaned out, snuffing the smoke, trying to see the pillaging and burning of the revolving villages, to catch the faint alarms, but hears only the

beat of the rails *heatherylarm heatherylarm heatherylarm.* Past sooty terraces into Liverpool Street.

*on the nativity of St Mary came Olaf and Sweyn
Forkbeard to London with 94 ships, and kept up un-
ceasing attack on the city...*

Hefting the mallet and cold chisel after breaking
open the wooden crates, overalled assistants waiting
to receive the canvases, the walls trembling in their
nudity. He had unpacked them in reverse order of
packing a month before, when he had plunged them
into sawdust like headstones.

Each canvas a layer of his life, flayed and tidied up.
And if one were sold, he had painted a copy to staunch
the loss. But still the time was lost to him. Until finally
he was spent, nailed into an insufferable present.

He needed a past. And if his own were used up,
then another's. And chancing upon a school book ac-
count of Olaf's adventures, had bought a translation of
the *Anglo-Saxon Chronicles.* And so he had followed,
with detours, his paintings.

When the last one was hung he left. He rode a tram
the length of the Strand. The current crackled through
the antennae in the humid air. He thought of light-
ning, Thor.

He didn't wait for the reviews, obituaries in fact, but left London for the Chilterns. He toured the villages, trying to pick up the long-dead scent, and so came to Oxford, expectant, walking, still hopeful, down Cornmarket Street, and entered the church of St Wulfric, its studded door resisting, and up, two stairs at a time, the tower to the carved relief, his fingers searching in the gloom for the figures, kneeling, and the poised sword, but worn, smooth, too smooth, and his nails slid on damp stone. And he stamped down the stairs, banging the door *and burned down the borough, and made their way on both sides of the Thames towards their ships. Then when they had been warned that levies were waiting to oppose them at London, they crossed at Staines...*

Down there the landing place. The water would have surged, it being winter. And the bridge would have been makeshift, treacherous. A mere succession of beams, rain-frotted.

To be later strengthened, repaired with oaks from Windsor Forest, demolished and rebuilt after the Civil War, surviving the one month's lifespan of the first stone bridge, then the cracking of the single span of iron, until – now? Gone. Demolished and burnt. Baedeker had lied. He stands now stolidly on stone, on the granite bridge of the Rennies and, dyspeptic, starts to fret. Stamping, heels ringing on the flagstones.

I need wood. I need the give and grain, the resonance of resin. Girls On The Bridge, Women On The Bridge – wooden bridges, all of them.

Woodcuts too, his most expressive medium. The texture beneath his fingers, the figures emerging fibrous from the plank, looming into being, solid in the depth of grain. Not scratched on wax, rolled on to the paper under the weight of stone. Not daubed on to canvas with less depth than the layer of varnish.

I should have been a Michelangelo. I could chip and gouge my creatures into life, into full roundness of being. Recall too the dead into a more fitting existence. Jørgen, say. Wouldn't he have a stronger hold among the living were he modelled in quartz than scrawled in oil? Their easels had locked, nearly toppled, on the field day in Lillestrøm with so little flat ground. They had laughed and linked arms and painted left-handed until recalled to sternness. And when the light failed they had swum together, Jørgen shaking his hair like a dog. So little a life. But with an extra dimension would he perhaps claim a greater share, claim more than his thirty-three years, come to strip him of memories they hadn't shared? Link his arm, jog his easel as a master as well as a student?

And the rest, Mother, Johanna – if their claims were unlimited would he have anything left? But **the past is merely the currently-present text; we cannot extend backwards the now**

Down there the landing stage.

Chill smoke from damp fires. Misted palaver, the occasional electric laugh. He strains to hear it, hear their plans, tactics lazily tossed around with the chewed bones, lust hibernating. He screws his eyes, already aching, against the pubs and cottages to blot them out, clear the scene. But the white walls are still there indelible on his retina.

As is Inger on his mind. Too much with him. Almost to the end. He couldn't paint her again, not yet. **I paint not what I see but what I saw. And I still see her. Always with me. In time, give me time.** And when he has painted her for the last time, dismissing her shade, what then shall he have? What last tatters **nothing outside the text, nothing beyond the text but texts** clock and bed.

He turns again to the riverbank, peering, knuckles whitening on the balustrade, temples pulsing.

The buildings are slowly disappearing, the white, the lights, all vanishing into

Fog. It swirls and thickens. He sees it as a miracle. The flies of history changing for him. He awaits the footlights at the water's edge. Dulled Norsemen moving by firelight, Olaf and Forkbeard shadowed by spotlight.

The street lamps are lit.

The fog coagulates, blanks out ten centuries, and ten before that. He peers, strains. His eyes flicker in nystagmic effort. The street lamp behind him sends out a banner of light reflected red by the fog as it presses in like glass, pressing him in like glass, squashing him in, and he **obdurate attempts to maintain an outmoded legibility – still vestigially permeating the art world – results in, can only result in, an ungraspable incommensurability which negates itself in**

CONFINGO

confingopublishing.uk